The Gryphon Press

—a voice for the voiceless—

These books are dedicated to those who foster compassion toward all animals and who practice ecological stewardship.

Our sincere thanks to Debbie Reynolds
for setting us on this remarkable flight path

For their support of *A Warbler's Journey,*
our heartfelt gratitude to
Emily Anderson, Patricia Bacchetti,
Nancy Gibson/Ron Sternal, David Hartwell,
James P. Lenfestey, Debbie Reynolds, and Brenda Wehle

———————————

Text set in Plantagenet Cherokee by Bookmobile Design and Digital Publisher Services
Printed in Canada

Library of Congress Cataloging-in-Publication Data
CIP data is on file with the Library of Congress

ISBN: 978-0-940719-47-7

1 3 5 7 9 10 8 6 4 2

———————————

I am the voice of the voiceless:
Through me, the dumb shall speak;
Till the deaf world's ear be made to hear
The cry of the wordless weak.

—from a poem by Ella Wheeler Wilcox, early 20th-century poet

A Warbler's Journey

Written by Scott Weidensaul

Painted by Nancy Lane

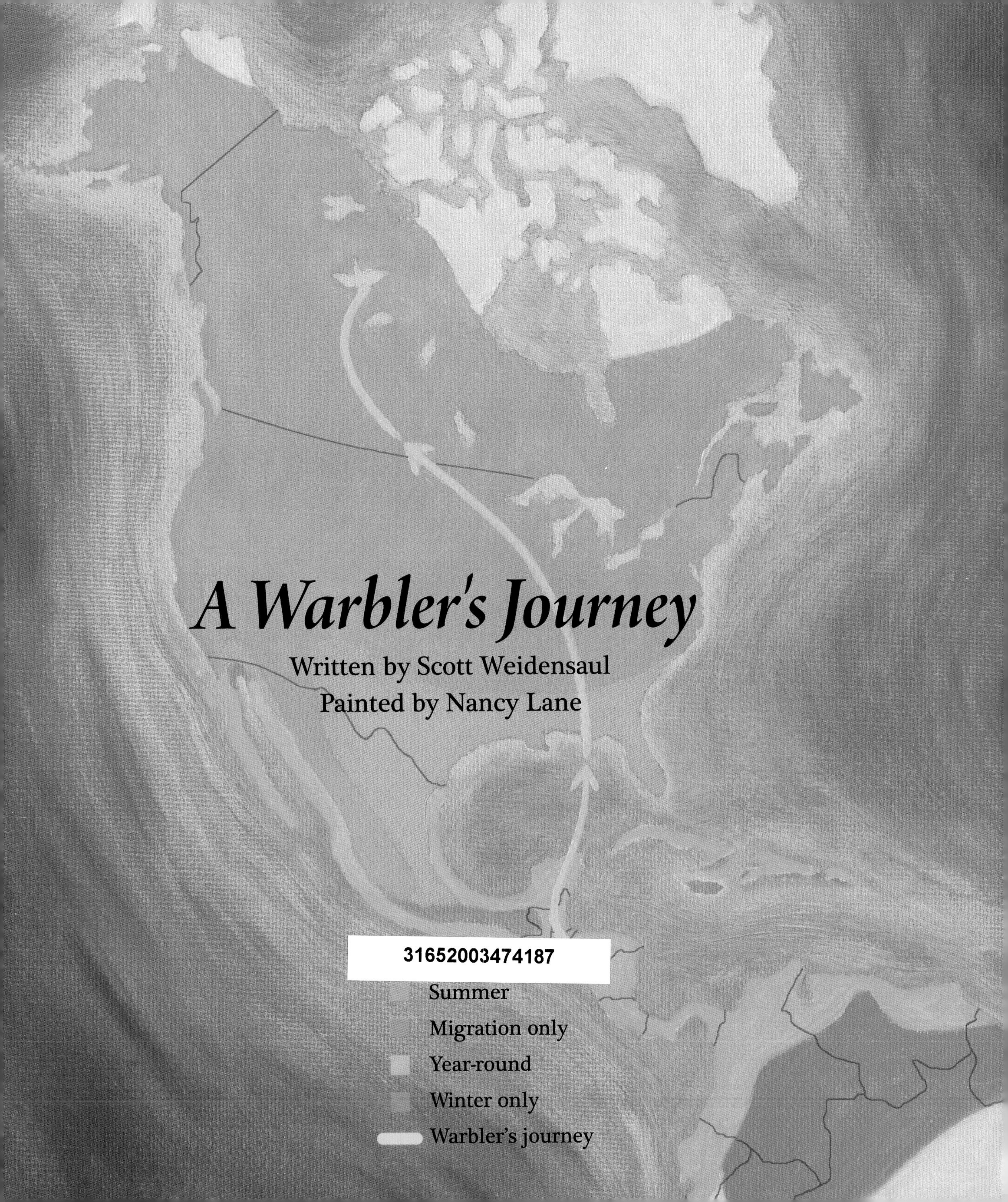

Summer

Migration only

Year-round

Winter only

Warbler's journey

The small yellow bird slept.

Around her, the tropical night air was warm and steamy. Snakes slithered. Bats swooped on leathery wings. Insect sounds filled the darkness but never disturbed the little warbler. Neither did the deep, long roar of the howler monkeys in the high treetops, loud as angry lions.

These were just the sounds of the forest. The sounds of home.

Daylight came and the warbler, the color of a ripe lemon, woke. She drank rainwater cupped in the base of a leaf, ate three caterpillars one after another, then darted to the edge of the forest, where the first rays of sunshine made the flowers glow.

For five months she had lived in this rain forest, through hot days and warm nights. But something inside her was different today, twitchy and excited.

She ate and ate and ate some more— soft bugs, little ripe berries—always eating but never really feeling full.

The girl's eyes fluttered and opened. The crowing of the family rooster had nudged her awake, as it did every morning. Today, though, something was different—and then she remembered: no school! It was the end of the harvest, and she needed to help her family gather the last of the coffee on their *finca* in the mountains.

Soon she and her brothers and sisters, her parents, and her *abuelito* and *abuelita* were walking slowly in the cool shade of the forest, picking the ripe coffee.

Butterflies gathered in colorful clusters. A hummingbird buzzed past her ear. Parakeets screeched overhead, a blur of bright colors.

A little yellow bird flew ahead of her, darting through the shadows.

"That is the *reinita amarilla*," said her grandfather. "They come from the north in November, just as the harvest begins, and they leave again now, in March, as we finish."

"Do they come for the coffee?" she asked her *abuelito*.

"No, no, *niña*, they eat the insects that hurt our coffee trees."

All day, the warbler's excitement grew. Finally, as the sun went down, she could no longer contain it, and she flew—not to her snug little roost in the forest, but up through the treetops, out into the darkening sky. She flew north.

All that night she flew, and she flew every night for the next week. She came at last to the ocean, where pale sand edged the Gulf of Mexico. She knew, deep inside, she needed to fly over that water, but she also knew she was not yet ready. She waited.

Two days. Three days. Five days. The little yellow bird searched constantly for food, knowing she would need every bite. Under her feathers she grew plump and heavy.

A week after arriving in the Yucatán, her body told her the time was right. The wind blew north, away over the blue gulf water. As the sun set, she followed the wind.

She flew all night, with brilliant stars
to point her north. All around her,
invisible in the dark, she heard the
voices of thousands of others migrating
north as well.

She flew as the sun rose
beyond her right wing, and flew on as
it sank, fiery and orange, beyond her
left wing.

It was like a race with no finish line
and no place to rest. But she was
strong. This was what she was meant
to do. The strength of her ancestors
was in her wings.

She flew as lightning streaked the darkness, as a cold wind blew hard in her face and rain soaked her feathers. Lower and lower she flew, as the dark, dangerous ocean grew closer.

She was tired, but she was strong. This was what she was meant to do.

In the peaceful dawn beyond the storm, the wind smelled like land. But below her, she saw only buildings and roads and yards of plain grass.

She could find no welcoming place, until she saw a splash of shady green and fluttered down among cool, lush trees and flowers.

She folded her wings and rested.

The boy woke. He dressed and ran outside, where Grandma was already working in the warm earth. He loved the colors and the smells of her backyard, where flowers and shrubs crowded in on all sides and water bubbled in a little pool.

"Here, now, help me plant this cardinal flower," she said, placing the roots in the hole as he covered them with damp soil. "This summer, the hummingbirds will love its red flowers."

He saw a flash of color. "Is that a hummingbird?" he asked.

"No," Grandma said. "That's a yellow warbler, the first one I've seen this spring. She must have just arrived, flying all the way from Mexico across the ocean. Imagine that!" Grandma shook her head in wonder, but the bird paid them no attention. The yard was full of good things to eat, and she was very, very hungry.

The warbler flew north each night for weeks, following the edge of spring as it pushed back winter. She rested once in a deep swamp, where alligators swam and barred owls hooted their crazy calls.

Farther north, in farm country, she slept in pasture thickets, where foxes yipped.

Eventually, the trees became a blanket of pointy spruce and dark firs, beneath which moose snorted and snuffled. The little warbler slept undisturbed. These were just the sounds of the forest. The sounds of home.

As she flew on, the trees became fewer and fewer, and the air still had the bite of late winter.

Patches of snow lay in the shadows, but the sun carried spring in its warmth. The warbler knew she was getting close.

When the last morning came, she saw below her a lake so wide she could hardly see the other shore.

She knew this place. It was where she had been born, in a nest of woven grass and downy plant fluff. It was where she had built her own nests and raised her own chicks.

And it was here that her mate, with streaks of rusty red on his golden chest, would be waiting, singing: *Sweet-sweet-sweet-I'm-so-sweet!*

The girl woke, and as soon as her eyes were open, she remembered. It was the day of the big celebration! She and her parents crowded into the council building to cheer as their elected chief and ministers from the government signed the papers that made it official—the land that had supported the People for generations would be protected forever.

The deep, clear lake, where in summer her uncles and cousins set their nets for trout and whitefish, would be safe. So would the tundra hillsides, where she helped her mother and aunts collect delicious blueberries and cloudberries, and the rushing river, along which her father hunted caribou and musk oxen, whose meat kept them fed through the winter.

Walking home between her parents, she saw a small, yellow *iyesaze* dash into the willows alongside the lake.

Another bird, even more golden, sang from a nearby branch: *Sweet-sweet-sweet-I'm-so-sweet!*

The girl was glad the land was safe not just for her family and the People, but for the birds and all the animals.

The warbler knew nothing of parks or people. She knew only that she was where she was meant to be. As the sun set, wolves howled on the far ridge and her mate sang his song one last time: *Sweet-sweet-sweet-you're-so-sweet!*

These were just the sounds of the forest. The sounds of home.

Easy Ways for Everyone to Help Warblers (and All Migratory Birds)

This is the story of one yellow warbler who leaves her winter territory in the highlands of Nicaragua, travels north to the Yucatán Peninsula, and then flies nonstop for six hundred miles across the Gulf of Mexico, a journey of up to forty hours. With hundreds of millions of other birds, she pushes north up the center of the North American continent, following the "green wave" of spring vegetation. Having flown nearly four thousand miles, she returns to her nesting territory along Great Slave Lake in the Northwest Territories, there to mate and raise her babies. Hers is one migration out of many millions, each a miracle of tenacity and survival.

This journey of great risks and challenges is made even harder today by human changes that have severely eroded these birds' habitat. But there are many actions, large and small, each of us can take to ease the migratory passage of these birds.

☙ If you have a backyard, devote at least part of it to native flowers, trees, and fruit-producing shrubs, which provide critical food and shelter for migratory birds.

☙ Avoid using garden chemicals and pesticides in your yard that will injure or kill birds.

☙ Ask your city leaders to manage public parks and green spaces for bird habitat as well as for human recreation, and to adopt "Lights Out" measures in spring and fall to help birds avoid life-endangering collisions with lighted office buildings and skyscrapers. (For more information, visit audubon.org/bird-friendly-communities.)

☙ Get to know the birds that migrate through your area each year, bringing colors, songs, and connections from far-distant lands to your community. Join your local bird club or Audubon chapter to go on a bird walk, where you'll learn from enthusiastic experts.

☙ Put up a bird feeder, preferably one that doesn't spill seeds and attract rodents, to bring your neighborhood birds closer. The Cornell Lab of Ornithology is the best one-stop shop for information about all things birds and birding, and their free Merlin Bird ID app will help you identify birds by sight and song. (Visit www.allaboutbirds.org.)